To my mom,
the poet grandma
A.H.

To my beautiful wife
P.H.

Text copyright © 1994 by Amy Hest
Illustrations copyright © 1994 by Paul Howard

First U.S. edition 1994
Published in Great Britain in 1994
by Walker Books Ltd., London.

Library of Congress Cataloging-in-Publication Data
Hest, Amy.
Rosie's fishing trip / written by Amy Hest ;
illustrated by Paul Howard.—
1st U.S. ed.
Summary: Grandpa and Rosie spend the morning
fishing and Rosie learns that catching a fish is not
the most important thing.
ISBN 1-56402-296-X
[1. Fishing—Fiction. 2. Grandfathers—Fiction.]
I. Howard, Paul, 1967– ill. II. Title.
PZ7.H4375Ro   1994
[E]—dc20   93-28543

10 9 8 7 6 5 4 3 2 1

Printed in Hong Kong

The pictures in this book were done in watercolor.

Candlewick Press
2067 Massachusetts Avenue
Cambridge, Massachusetts 02140

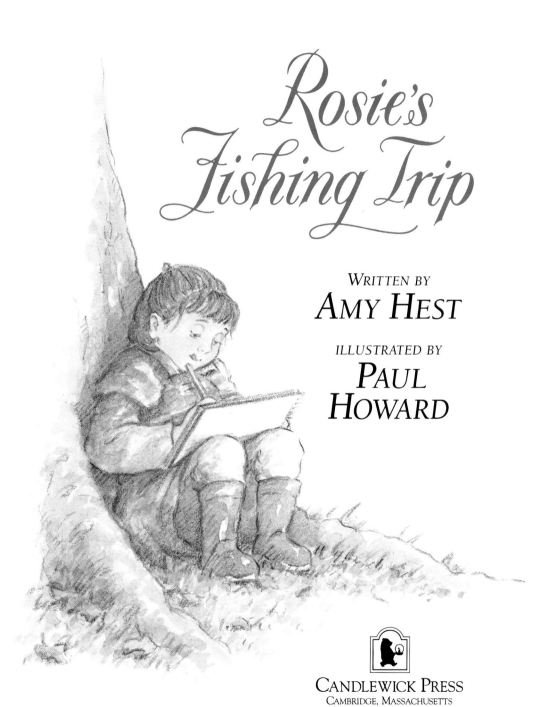

Rosie's Fishing Trip

WRITTEN BY
AMY HEST

ILLUSTRATED BY
PAUL HOWARD

CANDLEWICK PRESS
CAMBRIDGE, MASSACHUSETTS

Rosie's bicycle had two fat tires and a saddlebag in back. There was a wide wicker basket up front, and it was filling up fast with everything Rosie needed for her fishing trip, including three corn muffins and an old red thermos with chocolate milk inside.

Rosie wrapped her silver spoon in a cherry-colored napkin. She wrapped her tiny jar of jam in yellow tissue paper. She taped two pink pencils to her special drawing pad to make a picture, later, that would hang on someone's wall.

"Time to go fishing!" called Rosie.

"Good luck, my love!" Mama came to the kitchen to see her off. Her bathrobe was soft and green and smelled of dusting powder. (At night Mama liked curling up in her robe in her big chair near the window. Sometimes Rosie curled up too, and they took turns reading in a soft, night voice.)

Rosie's fishing coat had a cape across the back and seven slender buckles that buckled up the front.

Mama kissed both her cheeks.

Then Rosie bumped her bicycle down
the steps all the way to Front Street,
where it was still dark. Rosie shivered.
She did not much care for the dark.

But she did care for fishing and of
course for Grampa, who was waiting
on a corner near the park.

Rosie sucked in. She let her breath out.

Pedal, Rosie, pedal! There were too many shadows in the village in the morning. It was chilly and there was mist in the air, or maybe it was drizzle. *Pedal, Rosie, pedal!*

In between big houses and others
that were small, the sun was trying to
light up the town. *I am racing you, sun,
and I will win the race to Grampa!* Rosie
pedaled hard and she pedaled very fast,
stopping short at each cross street.

Grampa was waiting on a corner
near the park. Rosie rode and he walked
along with his big fishing bucket and
his tall fishing pole. They rode
and walked all the way to
Periwinkle Pond.

Rosie leaned her bicycle against a
tree. Grampa draped a cloth on a grassy
spot nearby. They each ate a muffin with
strawberry jam. Then they shared another.

"Tell me a poem, Grampa, and please
make it rhyme," said Rosie.

Grampa shook the thermos to make
a million chocolate bubbles that popped
on Rosie's nose.

"A poem about me is a good idea."

Sometimes Grampa said a poem
that spilled right out. Other times
they had to wait. Sometimes Grampa
scratched words on paper. Other times
he plucked words from air.

While they waited for a poem, they
went down to the pond and into the
pond way past their ankles. Grampa's
fishing boots were high to his knees.
Rosie's fishing boots used to be her
mother's. (They were still too big in
the toes, but she loved them anyway.)

Grampa held the pole over the pond.
They waited for fish. Rosie held the
pole too, but it was heavy, and still
no fish. *Come-on-fish-come-on!*

When Rosie's legs were tired, she leaned
against a tree and made a beautiful picture
of Grampa fishing in the pond in the mist

in the morning. She sketched a dog, too.
Rosie liked to draw dogs. And Grampa
liked to hang the pictures on his wall.

After a long, long time Grampa's fishing pole curved. Then it bounced. Rosie's heart bounced too. *Fish beware!* She reeled in the line. *You feel big, fish, but Rosie is strong!* She jiggled the line. *I'm going to get you, fish, and bring you home to Mama to cook you up for lunch!* Rosie reeled that fish right out of the pond.

The fish looked at Rosie and
Rosie looked back. He was small,
like a fist, and wriggly and scared.

They tossed him back and he swam
away with his cousins.

So-long-fish-so-long!

Rosie and Grampa rode and walked
through the village. There wasn't a
single fish in the bucket, but they
didn't mind. Grampa was thinking up
a poem, and Rosie was helping with
the rhymes. The sun came out and
the sky cleared up, and Mama kissed
everybody on both cheeks.

Lunch was waiting. They each had
a bowl of pasta. Afterward there
was ice cream with rainbow
sprinkles. And after
that, Grampa said
their poem:

Rosie's Fishing Trip

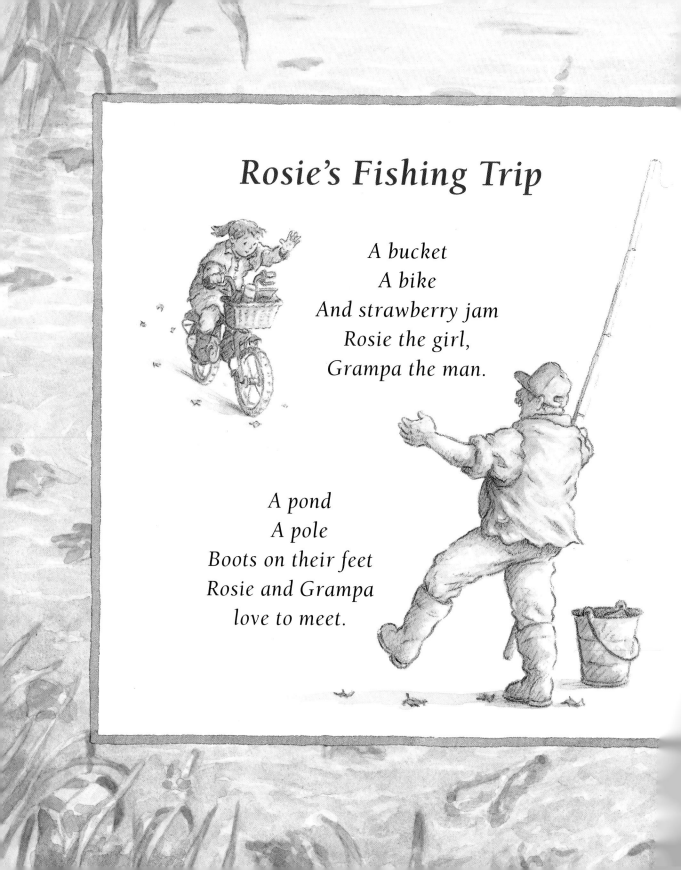

A bucket
A bike
And strawberry jam
Rosie the girl,
Grampa the man.

A pond
A pole
Boots on their feet
Rosie and Grampa
love to meet.